Moonlight Travelers

Story by Hugh Plant • Illustrated by Sarah Kenyon Nygaard

Beaver's Pond Press, Inc.

Edina, Minnesota

For Christopher, Jonathan and Thomas

In Memory of Dana DelBosco

Illustrated by Sarah Kenyon Nygaard

ISBN-13: 978-1-59298-173-1
ISBN-10: 1-59298-173-9

Library of Congress Catalog Number: 2006939765

Printed in the United States of America

First Printing: March 2007

11 10 09 08 07   5 4 3 2 1

Beaver's Pond Press, Inc.

7104 Ohms Lane, Suite 216
Edina, MN 55439
(952) 829-8818
www.BeaversPondPress.com

To order, visit www.BookHouseFulfillment.com
or call 1-800-901-3480. Quantity discounts available.

Not so very long ago, in a place not so very far away, lived Pig Girl.
She lived in a comfortable small house with big windows.

Pig Girl lived next to her good friend, the Music Man. Often, Pig Girl would listen while the Music Man made beautiful sounds with his music machines.

While the Music Man slept,
Pig Girl liked to visit her friends
who lived elsewhere in her
neighborhood.

This night Pig Girl planned to meet
with several friends who lived at the
end of the block.

As the moon rose in the sky, Pig Girl
climbed through the door on the top
of her house, lowered her ladder to the
ground, and scurried down the block to
Buckminster's house.

Buckminster was quite smart and liked learning about everything. He lived with the Maker of Things.

During the day,
Buckminster would
watch while the Maker
of Things made all sorts
of wonderful moving
contraptions that rolled
on the ground or whirled
through the air.

"So good to see you!" exclaimed
Buckminster when he first caught
sight of his friend Pig Girl.

"I have just returned from a trip to visit our good friend, Mr. Lopps,
who has been very ill, and to my surprise he was not home."

"I know Mr Lopps has been ill," said Pig Girl, "but he's always home."

"I'm very worried," said Buckminster.

"Then we must go find him," said Pig Girl.

"Yes, we must," agreed Buckminster. "But how?"

Pig Girl pondered the question. "Maybe we need a traveling machine! Like the great traveling machines your friend, the Maker of Things, is always building."

"Hmmm, yes," said Buckminster. "An interesting proposal. I could build us a traveling machine. But I wouldn't know how to drive it."

"What about Baby?" said Pig Girl. "He has been on many travels. Maybe he could be the driver."

"Very good idea," said Buckminster. "Let's go speak with Baby."

So Pig Girl and Buckminster set off for Baby's house.

Baby lived a short distance away on a farm with his friend, the Player. All day long Baby remained very still, never blinking an eye. Even on his many travels he never spoke or moved in any way. However, when the sun went down, Baby walked and talked and moved about just like anyone else. He considered it his job to watch over all the other animals on the farm during the night.

When Pig Girl and Buckminster arrived at the farm, Baby was, as always, watching over the other animals.

"Hey Baby," whispered Pig Girl. "Buckminster and I have a problem and we think that you might be able to help us."

"Well, what's the problem?" asked Baby as he wiggled out from under the Player's arm.

"Quite simply, it is this," said Pig Girl. "Mr. Lopps is missing, and we are afraid he may be lost somewhere. We must go look for him."

"Whoa!" said Baby. "How will we do this?"

"I will build us a great traveling machine like those that the Maker of Things builds," replied Buckminster. "It will be ready tomorrow night. We thought that perhaps you might be the driver."

"No problemo," said Baby, "I have been on many travels with my friend the Player in the Grand Driving Machine and have watched closely how it works. I'm quite sure that I could drive your machine."

"However," continued Baby, "this could be a very long journey which could take us far from home. How would we find our way back?"

"I know," said Pig Girl, "I will make music just like the Music Man does and bring it in the music box. We will leave a trail of musical notes behind us which will show us the way back home."

Agreeing that they each had much to do to prepare for their trip, Baby returned to his post alongside his sleeping friends, while Pig Girl and Buckminster went back to their homes.

That night Buckminster drew up plans for a fabulous traveling machine. It had wings high and low, a big propeller, a powerful engine, and seating for three. He worked all night locating the right parts and assembling the craft.

The next day Pig Girl was busy making music,

and Baby paid close attention to the controls of each machine
he encountered in his travels with the Player.

Night came and with it a large full moon, twinkling stars and warm clear air. The Magnificent Traveling Machine was complete. The three friends were ready to search for Mr. Lopps.

Baby whispered, "All on board… ready to roll?"

"Ready to roll," answered Pig Girl and Buckminster.

"Okay, here we go," whispered Baby. And with that he started the motor and drove the Magnificent Traveling Machine out the window and into the warm night air.

At first Baby steered the Magnificent Traveling Machine a little too high, then a little too low. Then he got it just right.

"I knew you could do it," said Pig Girl.

"This is really cool!" said Buckminster.

"No problemo," said Baby.

And so the search for Mr. Lopps began. The three friends flew high and low above the nighttime countryside.

They flew by a big red barn, around a large pine tree and under a long stone bridge, but no Mr. Lopps.

They flew over houses and
stores and baseball fields and
railroad tracks and cornfields.

They flew across a big blue
lake, past a waterfall and
beyond, but no Mr. Lopps.

Suddenly, out of the night, a strange winged creature appeared.

"Who are you?" asked Pig Girl.

"My name is Old One," answered the creature as he stretched out his wings and glided alongside the Magnificent Traveling Machine.

"We are looking for our friend, Mr Lopps," said Buckminster. "Have you by chance seen him?"

"Yes, I have. But Mr. Lopps is someplace where you cannot go."

"Oh, but we must see our friend," said Pig Girl. "We have been very worried about him."

Old One blinked. "You have journeyed far to find your friend. Therefore, tonight we shall grant an exception to the laws of the forest. You may visit Mr. Lopps, but only for a brief moment. Travel into the cave at the base of the giant tree up ahead. But remember… be quick. You must be back in the time that it takes the stars above to twinkle one hundred times."

So Baby steered the Magnificent Traveling Machine around the giant tree, going lower and lower until they were headed straight toward the cave.

"Whoa!" said Baby. "Here we go."

"Mr. Lopps, here we come," said Pig Girl.

"Hold on tight," said Buckminster.

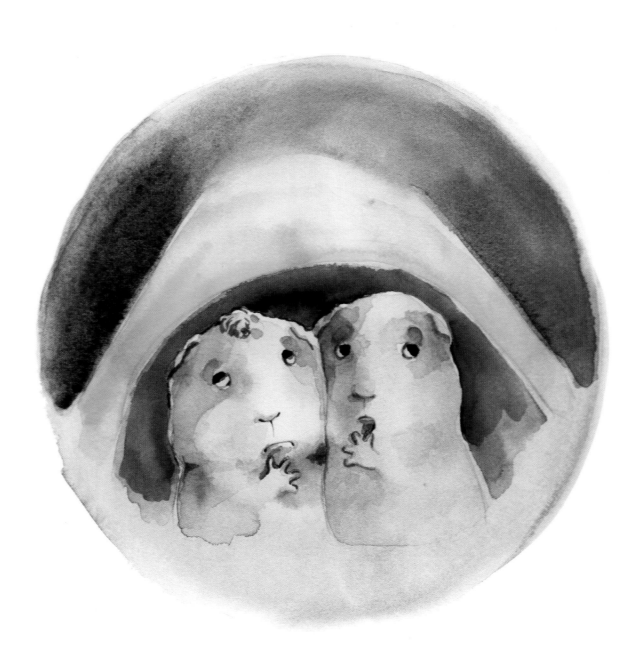

The Magnificent Traveling Machine swooped into the big dark cave.

"Oh, it's very dark in here," said Pig Girl. Suddenly…

the Magnificent Traveling Machine was out of the cave and flying through a beautiful canyon. The sun was out. A clear blue stream burbled and babbled its way along the canyon bottom. Big trees stood alongside the stream and spread upward along the canyon walls. Flowers danced in a gentle breeze.

The Magnificent Traveling Machine floated down out of the sky and settled onto a grassy meadow next to the stream.

"Wow!" said Pig Girl. "What a beautiful place this is."

"Where are we?" said Baby.

"I don't know," said Buckminster. "I'm afraid we might be lost."

"No, look," said Pig Girl, just as a small group of lop-eared rabbits appeared at the edge of the meadow.

"Mr. Lopps," called Pig Girl. "Mr. Lopps, is that you?"

One of the lop-eared rabbits rose up on his hind legs with his eyes wide in surprise.

"Cowabunga!" said Baby. "It's Mr. Lopps."

"Yahoo!" said Buckminster.

And with that, Pig Girl, Buckminster and Baby scurried across the meadow to greet their long-lost friend, Mr. Lopps.

"My goodness, it's so good to see my three friends again," said Mr. Lopps.

"We are so glad to find you," said Pig Girl.

"We were very worried about you," said Buckminster.

"How did you get to this place?" asked Baby.

"I'm not sure," said Mr. Lopps. "I don't remember much about my last night at my old home. I was very, very ill and stopped breathing. Then Old One appeared and brought me to this beautiful valley. I have a nice new home, have met some new friends and I am happy. In this place everything is the same as before, yet everything is different."

Just then a sudden gust of wind flattened the tall grass in the meadow, and with it came the voice of the Old One: "It is time."

"Quick!" said Mr. Lopps. "Back to your traveling machine. You must leave at once. It is not your time to be here."

Baby, Buckminster and Pig Girl climbed back aboard the Magnificent Traveling Machine.

"I'm glad we found you, Mr. Lopps," said Buckminster.

"I'm glad that you are happy," said Baby.

"We will miss you," said Pig Girl.

"Good-bye," said Mr. Lopps, waving his paw. "And remember, we will always be friends."

Baby started the engine
and drove the Magnificent
Traveling Machine across the
meadow and up into the sky.

The three friends flew back through the dark cave and out into the moonlit sky. Baby
steered the Magnificent Traveling Machine up higher and higher around the giant tree.

"No time to waste," said Old One as he stretched out one wing and pointed the way.
"Time to go home."

So Baby, Buckminster and Pig Girl waved good-bye to Old One and flew on –

past a burbly stream, around the big trees, over a hill, and on out of the forest. Their trail of musical notes still hung in the air.

They flew past a waterfall and across a big blue lake.

They flew over cornfields and railroad tracks and baseball fields and stores and houses.

They flew under a stone bridge, around a large pine tree, and by a big red barn.

They flew low
and high above
the countryside
until there it was – home.

In through the window they
went. Baby circled once over the
sleeping Maker of Things and lightly
touched down alongside Buckminster's house.

"Excellent trip," said Buckminster.

"Excellent landing," said Pig Girl.

"No problemo," said Baby.

And so the three friends lived happily on.
There were more adventures to follow,
machines to be built,
and music to be made.
And often when the sun went down and the moon came up, the three friends would get together and talk about what they had learned that day. And sometimes when a gentle breeze rustled the warm night air, they would hear the voice of Mr. Lopps saying, "Remember, we will always be friends...forever and ever."

The
End

About the Author

Hugh Plant, a lover of animals and the outdoors, is a native of Minneapolis, Minnesota. A child's grief over the death of a family pet inspired him to write this story. He is an avid skier, river rafter, fisherman, hiker, and mountain biker. He currently lives and works in the Rocky Mountains.

About the Illustrator

Sarah Kenyon Nygaard lives in Minnesota with her husband Harlan and two daughters, Chelsea and Michelle. A lifelong love of children's books led her to pursue a career as an illustrator for children's stories.